SNOW DRILL

P9-DZL-794

A long time ago in a galaxy far, far away, there was a war between the Empire and the rebels. The Empire was constantly searching for the rebels, because they were always hiding! How many carrots can you see? Can you also find a lightsaber?

TRACKING TRAILS

Only a daring traveller would venture into the sands of Tatooine . . . so what's C-3PO doing there? He's searching for his friend R2-D2, who has disappeared. If the golden droid follows his tracks he should be able to find him. Which trail belongs to R2-D2?

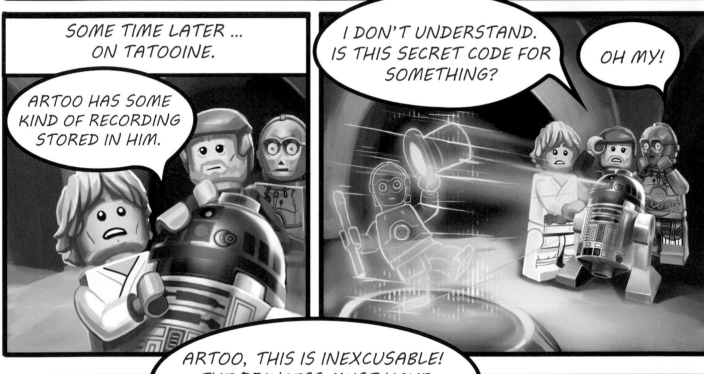

THE HEAT IS ON

Han and Luke must deliver the plans of the Imperial Death Star to the rebels on Alderaan! The symbol that appears the most in the table is the one that marks the exact location of the planet.

HAN, DID YOU PACK THE SUNBLOCK? YOU MENTIONED IT GETS QUITE HOT ON ALDERAAN.

WHO'S THE WINNER?

Han's friend, Lando Calrissian, couldn't make it to the X-wing competition, so he sent a message to his friends. Read their replies opposite to find out who won the race.

X-WING RACE

LUKE SKYWALKER

WEDGE ANTILLES

JEK PORKINS

DUTCH VANDER

WHO WILL BECOME THE ACE OF THE SKIES? COME ALONG TO FIND OUT!

Free entry for all rebels. Vader and his kind – NO ENTRY!

ICY MESS

Imperial troopers have appeared on Hoth! Help this brave rebel get his equipment together. Find and circle the shelf where his items are laid out in the same order as they are shown in the box below.

HOW ARE WE SUPPOSED TO DEFEAT THE EMPIRE, IF WE CAN'T EVEN KEEP OUR SHELVES TIDY?

DARK DISCIPLINE

Look at the Imperial stormtroopers regrouping on the deck of the Death Star Imperial base. Try to work out which three troopers shown in the boxes below do not appear in the squad marching towards Vader.

A

B

C

D

YOU THERE, AT THE BACK, KEEP UP!

UNLUCKY PATROL

Luke found himself in a precarious position on one of the patrols. He was imprisoned by a savage wampa! Number the pictures from 1-4 to show exactly what happened to the young Jedi.

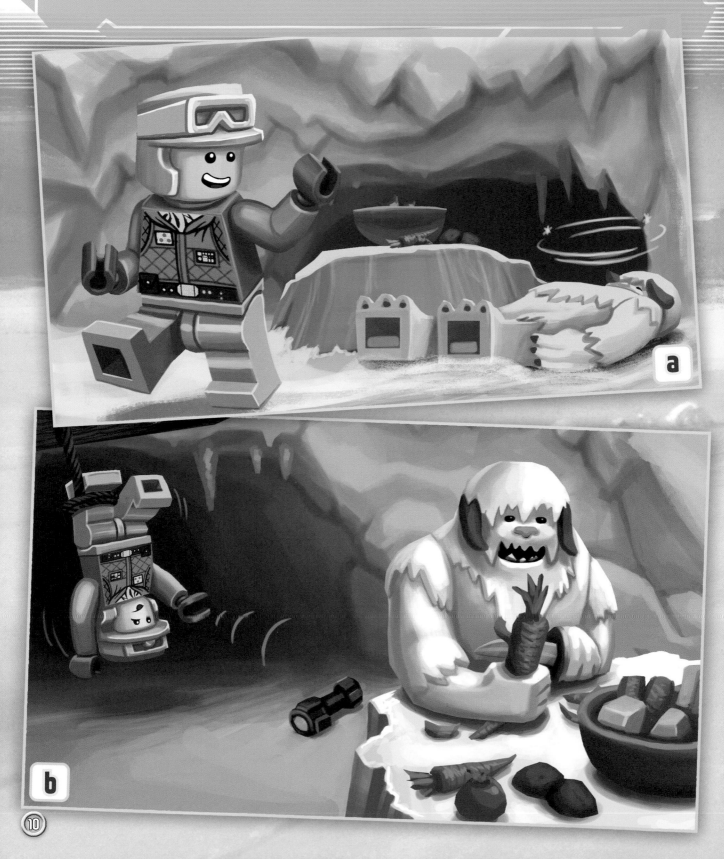

a

b

TWISTED TRAILS

The *Millennium Falcon* is on a secret mission. This time, its star trail is leading it to one of planet Endor's moons. Which hyperspace path should Han and Chewie take to reach their destination?

MY HEAD'S SPINNING FROM ALL THE POSSIBILITIES!

RUN, HAN!

When a price was put on Han Solo's head, he became a target for many greedy types. Lead him through the winding streets so he can reach his friends without encountering any bounty hunters.

WOAH, MY CHEST HURTS ... I SHOULDN'T HAVE SKIPPED SPORTS AT SCHOOL!

 = BOUNTY HUNTERS.

YODA'S WATCHFUL EYE

On the swampy planet of Dagobah, Master Yoda is training Luke to become a Jedi warrior. He just used the Force to pull out a few vehicles from the marshes! Can you match them to the impressions they left in the mud?

THREE OF THE VEHICLES HAVE SOMETHING IN COMMON, BUT THERE'S AN ODD ONE OUT. WHICH ONE IS IT?

GAME TIME

After a hard training session Luke needed a break, so Yoda decided to play his favourite game with him – Missing Domino! Which domino should Luke put in the empty space?

SOME BREAK THIS IS! I'D RATHER BE PULLING X-WINGS OUT OF THE MUD!

HIDDEN STORMTROOPER

Kylo Ren is preparing to launch an attack with his trusted First Order stormtroopers. However, one of them is not as trustworthy as the others! It's Finn! Can you spot him in the line-up? His armour is different from all of the others.

I'M GLAD I QUIT – I WAS GETTING FED UP WITH THIS BUCKET!

REFURBISHED FALCON

The *Millennium Falcon* has never looked better! It's thirty years old and still the best ride in the galaxy. Look at the small pictures and draw lines to show where each one should go.

AT THE SCRAPYARD

What's better than a fast and sturdy speeder? Two fast and sturdy speeders! That's why Rey decided to build another vehicle. Circle the 7 parts she needs to build a similar red machine. BB-8's spotted a discarded droid. Can you find it?

ROUGH FLIGHT

Poe Dameron has lost his way in an asteroid field. Help him find the route through it by drawing lines to join 1-9 and 9 to the FINISH. Then, draw arrows in the blue boxes below to show Poe which buttons to press to pilot his X-wing to safety.

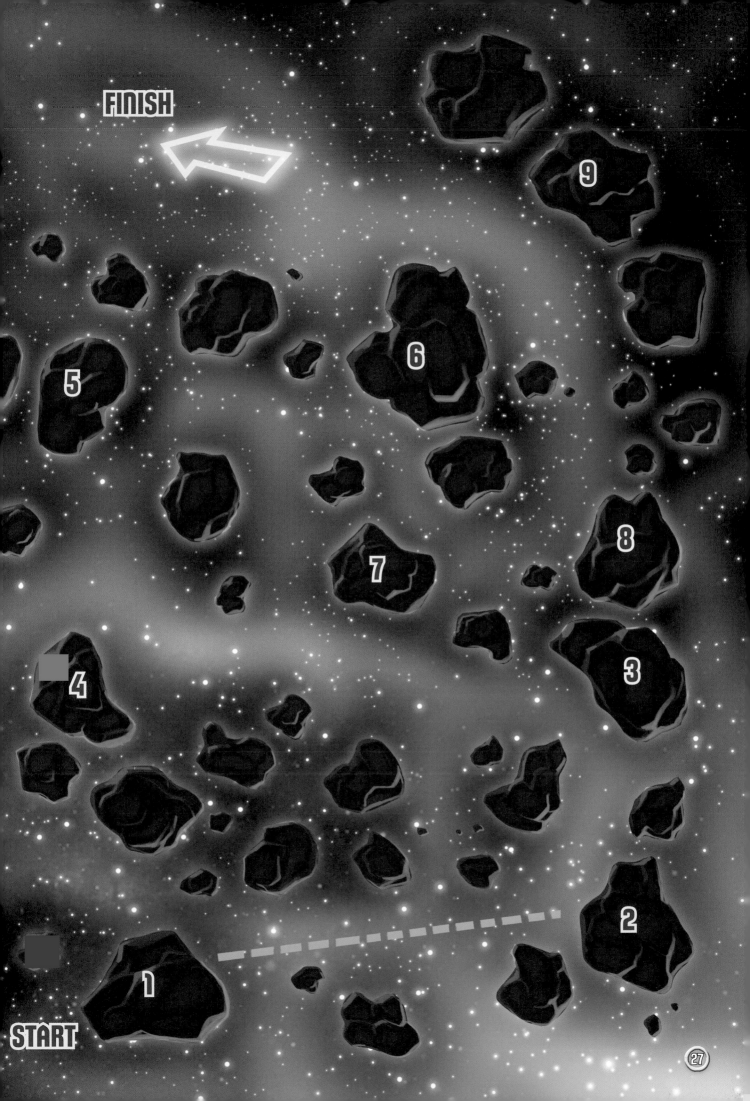

FINISH

9

5

6

8

7

3

4

2

1

START

STAR QUIZ

1. On what planet did Master Yoda train Luke Skywalker?
   a) Tatooine
   b) Dagobah
   c) Alderaan

2. What is the name of the Empire's huge battle station?
   a) The Deadly Star
   b) The Dread Star
   c) The Death Star

3. Who became a target for greedy galactic bounty hunters?
   a) Kylo Ren
   b) Rey
   c) Han Solo

4. Who is Leia Organa?
   a) a countess
   b) a queen
   c) a princess

5. What creature captured Luke in its cave?
   a) a tauntaun
   b) a wampa
   c) Lando Calrissian

6. What type of starship does Poe Dameron fly?
   a) an X-wing starfigher
   b) the *Millennium Falcon*
   c) a TIE fighter

7. What is the name of the evil organisation represented by Kylo Ren and his stormtroopers?
   a) The New Order
   b) The Bad Order
   c) The First Order

ANSWERS

Pg. 1

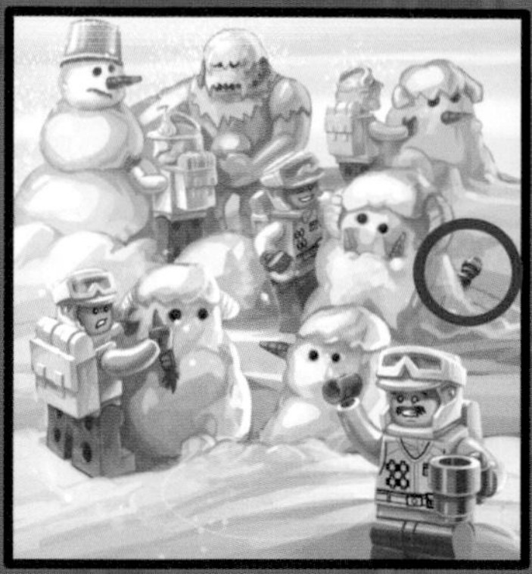

There are 6 carrots

Pg. 2

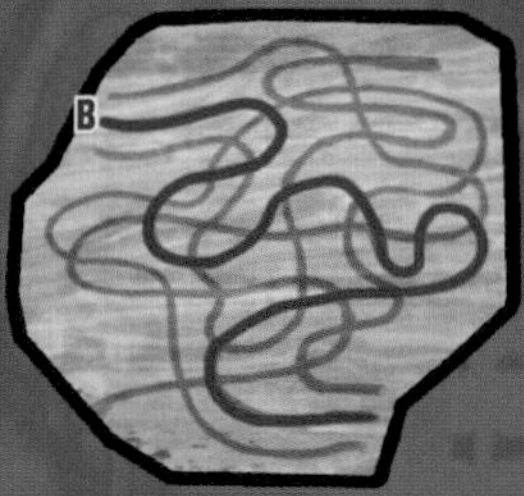

Pg. 4–5

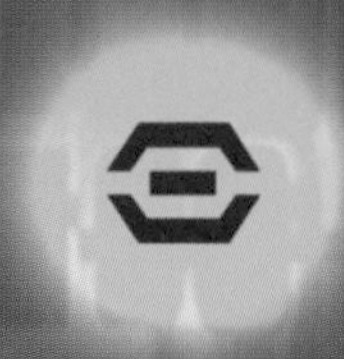

Pg. 6–7

Pg. 8

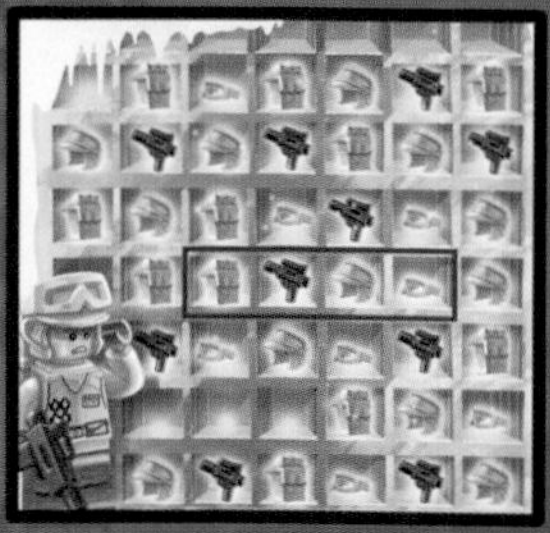

Pg. 9

D

Pg. 10–11

a – 4, b – 2, c –1, d – 3

Pg. 16–17

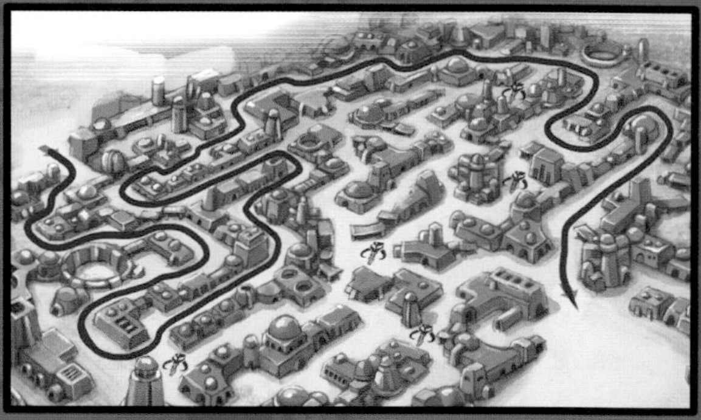

Pg. 12–13

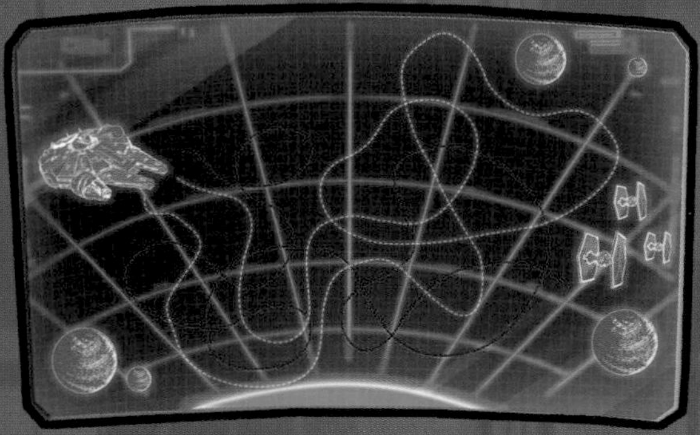

Pg. 18–19

A – 3, B – 1, C – 4, D – 2

TIE fighter is the only Imperial starship of the four

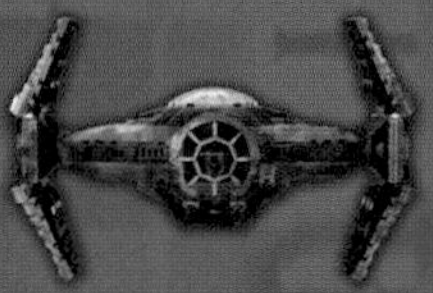

Pg. 20

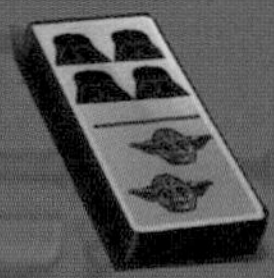

Pg. 21

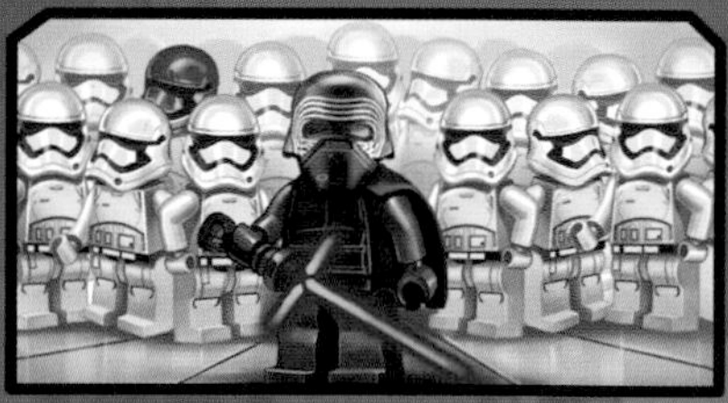

Pg. 22–23

1 – A, 2 – E, 3 – B, 4 – C, 5 – D

Pg. 24–25

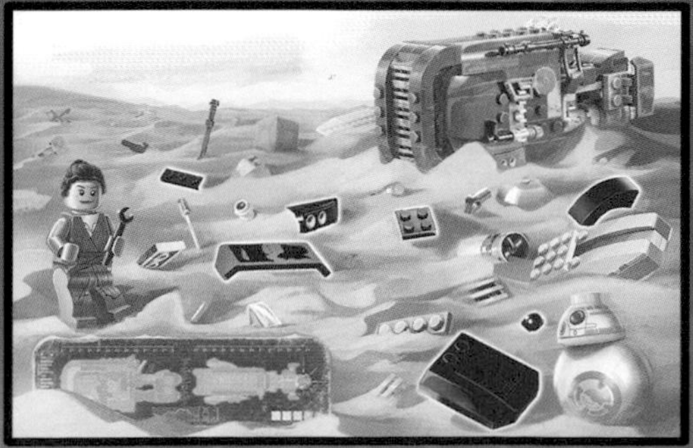

Pg. 26–27

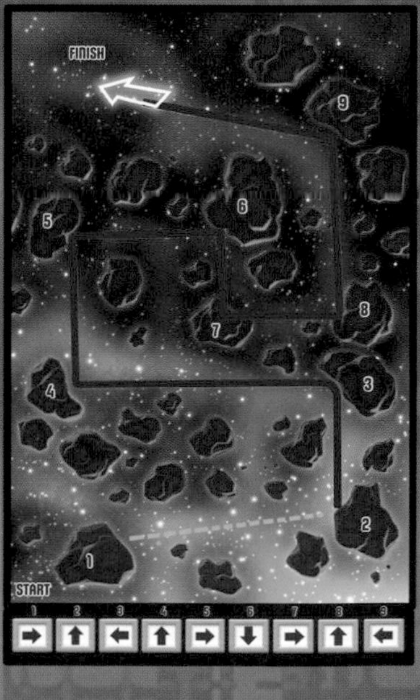

Pg. 28–29

1 – b

2 – c

3 – c

4 – c

5 – b

6 – a

7 – c

HOW TO BUILD
THE REBEL SOLDIER

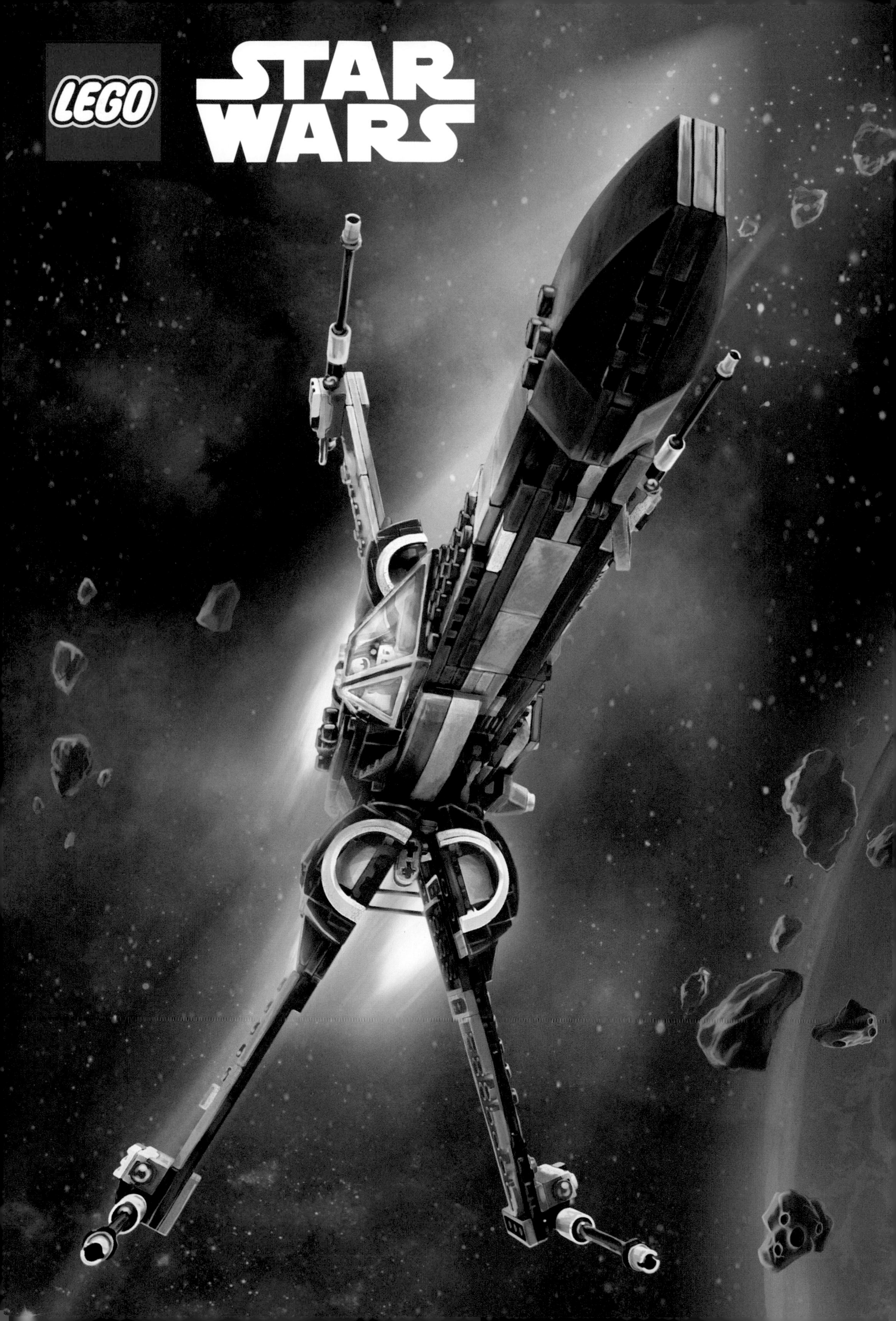
LEGO
STAR WARS